WHERE IN TIME IS CARMEN SANDIEGO?

Text by John Peel

Cover Illustration by Paul Vaccarello

Interior Illustration by John Nez

Western Publishing Company, Inc.,
Racine, Wisconsin 53404

Your Briefing

Congratulations — you've been hired as a rookie detective for the Acme Detective Agency. Your goal is to outsmart Carmen Sandiego and her gang by solving the cases in this book. Each time you solve a case and make the least amount of moves, you'll get a promotion.

There are four cases to solve in this book. To solve each case, start by removing the cards from the insert in the middle of this book. Divide the cards into four groups. You should have the following:

    4 Bookmark / Scorecards
    4 Stolen Object Cards
    8 Suspect Cards
    8 Subject Cards

Use a different **scorecard** for each game to write down clues and eliminate suspects. Each time you are told to go to a different number in the story, mark that move point on your scorecard. At the end of each game, add up the total points. Check your score on the last page to see if you've earned a promotion.

When you arrive in a new time period, use the same card as a **bookmark** to mark the place that you're in while you're investigating — sometimes you'll have to retrace your steps.

Each case involves a stolen object. Decide which case you are going to solve by picking a **stolen object card**. Put the other stolen object cards away until you are ready to solve those cases.

As you read each case you will be given clues about different suspects. Use those clues and the ones on the back of the **suspect cards** to decide which suspect you must capture. When you have made your decision, put the other suspect cards aside. The suspect card you have chosen serves as your warrant for the arrest.

Use the **subject cards** for information on the various time periods that you'll have to visit while tracking down a suspect. Put aside any cards that don't fit the clues you are given, until you have only one subject card left.

Be very careful when you read the clues. Think about them.

For example, suppose you are told that the crook wanted to read Moby Dick, and you discover that the book was written by Herman Melville, an American writer who lived from 1819-1891 and who wrote the book in 1851. This doesn't mean that the crook had to go to America, because books are published all over the world. Nor does it mean that the crook had to meet Melville. What it does mean is that the crook can't

4

have gone farther back in time than 1851, because that was the year the book was written. So you could rule out any times earlier than 1851.

The same thing applies to paintings and music — the crook can't have gone back to a time before they were painted or written, but he or she didn't have to meet the artist or musician.

Of course, you might be told that the crook wanted to meet Herman Melville, in which case he or she would have had to have visited America while Melville was alive. But if the person that the crook wanted to meet was either an explorer or a soldier, then he or she could have met that person either in their home country or in the one that they explored or fought in. Be especially careful here: some explorers went around the world, so you could meet them anywhere at all. Read all of your clues very carefully.

Ready? OK — put on your raincoat and hat and get ready to set off on another dangerous mission for the Acme Detective Agency. . . .

You're in your office at the Acme Detective Agency. You can hear the rain pounding on your windows, like the beat in a bad rap song. You glance up at the clock. Almost time for lunch. You wonder if you should stop in the small restaurant in the lobby for soup and a sandwich. The idea is not appealing — the restaurant's food is so bad you want to have the owner arrested on charges of attempted murder! But you don't feel like going out in the rainstorm just to get food. Decisions, decisions. . .

While you're thinking about lunch, the phone on your desk rings. You answer it. It's the Chief, sounding worried.

"Get into my office!" he yells into the phone. You do your best and are in the Chief's office in the blink of an eye. You slip into the chair facing him. The Chief's face looks as gray as his hair. As he tosses you a folder he grunts, "Four big thefts this time."

"Let me guess," you tell him. "Carmen Sandiego and her gang?"

"Yes," he says wearily. "We thought most of Carmen's gang was doing time in jail, but somehow a few gang members have managed to get hold of portable time machines and escaped. It seems they've are all jumped back to a time

6

before jails were built and then just walked away."

"Tough," you comment.

"It's worse than tough," he tells you. "They're starting a new crime wave throughout history. They've got to be stopped before they loot the incredible treasures of history. You've had the best luck capturing them in the past, so this is your case now. Go down to the lab and check out your portable time machine, the Chronoskimmer. Then get started right away."

Nodding, you leave his office. As you check out the Chronoskimmer, you also check out the stolen objects. Four of them . . . Well, the only thing to do is to pick out one, read the case, and follow the instructions to get to your first time period and place to look for clues. You're starving. You hope it's lunchtime whenever and wherever you arrive — and not raining.

If you've chosen to recapture:

The Leaning Tower of Pisa — go to 80
The Last Dodo Bird — go to 18
The Liberty Bell — go to 134
The Crown Jewels — go to 105

1. You've arrived in Italy in 1492. Though he's Italian, Christopher Columbus is discovering America this year — but he's doing it for Spain, not Italy. You're discovering that you've come to the wrong time and place. Better zip off to 17.

2. Your trip through time leaves you in Spain, 1498. The Spanish are driving out foreign invaders this year, and you soon find out that you're not welcome. Not only that, but there's no sign of the crook you're chasing. Better head to 17, fast.

3. You're on the trail of Nosmo King. The sewing machine will be invented in a few months. You hope to sew up this case before then. But King isn't around, and you're forced to go to 54.

4. Sitting Bull, a brilliant warrior, was a chief of the Teton Sioux. He led the Indian forces at the Battle of the Little Big Horn (1876), the battle that defeated General Custer. You ask him about the crook you're chasing.

"The black-haired man was here," the chief tells you. "He said he was going to meet a relative of the great Genghis Khan."

You thank Sitting Bull and head back to your base (106) to check out these clues.

5. You meet with a young Samuel Clemens, before he adopted his pen name of "Mark Twain." Some day he will write a number of great novels, including *The Adventures Of Tom Sawyer* and *A Connecticut Yankee in King Arthur's Court.* Right now, though, he's living in the town of Hannibal, on the Mississippi River. You ask him about the thief you're tracking.

"She was here," he tells you with a grin. "She told me that she was off to a country ruled by a queen."

You wish him well and leave him watching the river that will give him many ideas for stories.You head back to home base (71) to check out what he's told you.

6. You've arrived in the United States in the year 1829. It's a time when many people are moving out West, but there's no place here for you. You'd better move out to 17.

7. It would be difficult to find a more brilliant person in all of history than Leonardo da Vinci. He was a painter, a scholar, a scientist, and a man of wit and learning. He studied everything

with a sense of wonder, trying to discover how and why it worked. You wish that you had more time to talk with him, but you can only ask him about the thief you're tracking.

"Ah, yes," he tells you. "I remember him. A red-haired man. He said that he wanted to read *The Divine Comedy*."

With a sigh, you leave Leonardo to his thoughts and return to your Chronoskimmer (69) to check out these clues.

8. You've arrived in Chicago in 1930. It's not a good place to be, because rival gangsters are trying to take over the town. A false move in this city could leave you being tossed in the river with a pair of cement overshoes! But you're very careful, and you've tracked Pete Moss to a shady bar on the shore of Lake Michigan. He's playing pool with some low-life scum and bragging about getting away with the Liberty Bell.

"That's my cue," you say, grabbing his cue stick from him. One of the thugs with him goes for a gun, but you hit him hard with the stick. He drops his gun, and everyone moves slowly away from you.

"Okay, Pete," you tell the crook. "I'm from Acme. You heard of that?"

"Rings a bell," he says.

"Speaking of bells, Pete," you grin, "hand over the Liberty Bell. Then it can go back on display, and you can go back to jail. The game's over."

You take him out of the hall — and back to the future with you. Once there, the police haul Pete off and return the Liberty Bell to Philadelphia. You visit the Chief to let him know how things turned out.

"Great job," he tells you. "Why not head straight to the back of the book to see whether or not you've earned yourself that promotion?"

9. Your Chronoskimmer lands in England in the year 1718. It's a time of great change, with many scientists, writers, and thinkers living and working here. It's an exciting time to be alive, but you know you don't have time to spare. Checking your Chronoskimmer, you detect patterns in the time field. After a moment, the chronoskimmer's computer identifies them. The thief you're tracking met with three famous people. Maybe one of them can put you on the crook's trail!

If you want to talk to:
Sir Isaac Newton — go to 13
Daniel Defoe — go to 139
Blackbeard the Pirate — go to 91

10. It's the Sixties and the latest fad is the Hippie Movement. Long hair, torn jeans, and peace signs are in. What's out, sadly, is your thinking. Sybil Servant is nowhere to be found, so you have to pack up and head for 54.

11. William the Conqueror was the last person to successfully invade England. He and his men struck from France in 1066 and fought the forces of Harold near Hastings. The invasion was later commemorated by the famous Bayeux Tapestry, which is over 230 feet long. When you arrive, William is in a good mood, having won the battle, and you ask him about the thief you're after.

"Ah, the brown-eyed man," William muses. "He did say that he was going to see a performance of a play I've never heard of. *Romeo And Juliet*, I think he called it. Well, I've no time to play — I've a country to rule."

"Rule Brittania," you say as you return to your Chronoskimmer (105) to note these clues.

12. You've arrived in America in the year 1521. There are just a few Spanish settlements in what will become Florida. Ponce de Leon has failed in his search for the Fountain of Youth — and you've failed in your search for your culprit. Time to head to 17.

13. Sir Isaac Newton greets you as you arrive. By now he's extremely famous for his theory of gravity, for his work on the laws of motion, and for his Newtonian telescope. You compliment him on his work, and he offers to show you his latest telescope.

When you take a look in his study, you see a thief trying to steal the telescope! Quickly, you jump the man, and after a brief struggle, you're in deep trouble. He's an expert in kung-fu, and he throws you clean across the room. He's about to pounce on you again when you see Newton. He's picked up a paperweight from his desk, and after a quick calculation, he throws it. It hits the thief, knocking him out. Newton smiles.

"One advantage in having worked out the laws of motion," he tells you. "But I fear this villain will be out cold for hours yet."

"Thanks for the help, Isaac," you reply. "I'll just have to check one of my other leads. But it's quite clear I'm getting close to the thief!"

You put yourself in motion back to your Chronoskimmer (9) to check out the next clue.

14. You're in France, and the year is 1807. Napoleon Bonaparte has declared himself Emperor, and he and his armies have conquered a good

deal of Europe. National feelings run high, and you realize you might have trouble if your foreign

accent shows through your rusty French.

With a buzz, your portable chronoskimmer's computer finishes tracing the path of the thief. It seems she's done a little visiting here and has moved on to one of three possible destinations.

If you want to talk to:
Napoleon — go to 76
Alessandro Volta — go to 140
Alexandre Dumas — go to 39

If you're ready to travel to:
Spain in the year 1498 — go to 2
Italy in the year 1182 — go to 64
England in the year 1595 — go to 116

15. You reach the home of Washington Irving in upstate New York, the setting of many of his future tales. Right now, he's just seventeen years old, but one day he's going to write the tales of *Rip Van Winkle* and *The Legend Of Sleepy Hollow*. For these works, he will become the first world-famous American author. You greet him and ask about the thief you're tracking.

"He was here." Irving tells you. "Stopped for a drink of apple cider. He mentioned that he was going to try and get Michaelangelo's autograph."

Thanking him, you head back to base (161) to check out this clue.

16. Your Chronoskimmer has brought you to England in the year 1703. Many inventions are being made. Sadly, you're making your own discovery — that you'd better head straight to 17. Don't worry, it's not too far away!

17. Well, it's time to face the facts — you've followed a fake trail. The thief you're after isn't

here. Better head back to the last time period in which you had clues and recheck your deductions (you remembered to leave your bookmark there, didn't you?). Don't forget to add in the extra travel points for this wasted trip.

18. Mauritius is a small island off the coast of Africa. The island was first settled by the Portuguese in the sixteenth century, but then it was taken over by the Dutch, the French, and finally the English. The dodo birds that once lived here were killed to feed the crews of passing ships going from Europe to the Orient.

The chronoskimmer's computer in your Chronoskimmer beeps to tell you it's done its work. It seems that the thief you're after has stopped to see three people in this area. Then the crook traveled on. The chronoskimmer's computer tells you that it was to one of three possible times and places, so you'd better hope you can get some clues!

If you want to interrogate:

Jan van Riebeeck — go to 42

Mulay Ismael — go to 123

Maurice of Nassau — go to 155

If you think the thief went to:

France in the year 1422 — go to 143

America in the year 1850 — go to 71
America in the year 1780 — go to 34

19. Queen Elizabeth the First is an impressive woman, with bright red hair and a pale face. Wearing a huge dress that glitters with jewels, the queen greets you politely. A witty, brilliant lady, she was one of England's most beloved rulers and led the country in one of its greatest times. You ask her about the crook you're chasing.

"Ah, yes," she tells you. "That wretched woman was here. She was trying to steal some of my jewels. My men-at-arms tried to catch her to throw her in the Tower of London, but she gave them the slip."

"Do you have any idea where she went, your majesty?" you ask her.

"Well, she did say something about wanting to read a book. *King Solomon's Mines*, I believe she called it. If you find out where they are, perhaps you could tell me? Francis Drake has been after me to send him on another trip."

You smile and decide to go on a trip of your own, back to your Chronoskimmer (116) to check out this clue.

20. You've followed the trail of Heidi Gosikh to a small house in Paris. Here Daguerre is

working. He's invented the first working photographic process, and you wonder what he's developing. As it turns out, it's a false trail. It develops that you've been tricked. Time to head for 54.

21. You've arrived in America in the year 1776. The Revolutionary War is in full swing, with the American colonial army fighting the British. In the middle of all the shooting, you discover not only a bullet hole in your hat but also that you're in the wrong place. Head straight for cover — and 17.

22. Sir Arthur Sullivan is busily composing when you arrive at his house. He and his partner, W.S. Gilbert, have become famous for writing their comic operas *HMS Pinafore* and *The Pirates Of Penzance*. Right now, they're hard at work on their latest opera, *The Mikado*. Sullivan takes some time to talk with you, and you ask about the thief you're after.

"Yes, I recall her," he tells you. "A red-haired lady. She asked if she could play Ruth in *The Pirates Of Penzance*, and I told her we had already cast that part. She said that she was off to a place where she could read about radioactive things. Whatever that means."

You thank him for his help and leave him to

his composing. You make your way back to your Chronoskimmer (127) to check out these clues.

23. It's the Sixties, and rock and roll is all the rage. You've tracked Nosmo King to an Elvis Presley concert, but there are so many people here that there's no way you could ever check out the place. There's no sign of Nosmo King, and you leave The King — Elvis — to sing while you head for 54.

24. You've reached China in the year 1200. Temujin, the Mongol warlord, is ravaging the country. In six years he will be proclaimed the "great ruler," Genghis Khan. Right now, though, it's pretty obvious that this isn't the best place in the world to be. You move along to 17.

25. This is France in the year 1920. World War I has been over for only a couple of years, but France still shows signs of having been heavily battered. Workers are busy rebuilding the country, and no one has time to talk to you. You soon realize that you're in the wrong place, and you head for 17.

26. The steam pump was invented two years back, in 1716, but you've run completely out of

steam. Your hunt for Fast Eddie B has been fruitless, so you have to make your way to 54.

27. It's the year 1861, and you arrive in America. The American Civil War has just broken out, and this is definitely a dangerous place to be. Not only that, but there's no sign of your thief at all. You'd better head for 17 before you get your head blown off by a cannonball!

28. You've landed in England in the year 1575. It's a period of tension between England and Spain, because both countries are fighting for the same markets. It doesn't make much difference to you, though, because you find no trace of the thief you're hunting. You have to head for 17.

29. You've trailed Fast Eddie B to a speakeasy — a hidden bar set up during the time of Prohibition. But, you don't know the correct password and you're not allowed in. When you return with the police, the place is empty. Go to 54.

30. This is Spain in the year 1478. The two main provinces of Castile and Aragon are about to join to form the Spain that we now know. But none of this is much use to you. You're on the

wrong track here and have to head for 17.

31. You've arrived in Russia in 1892, a time of sweeping reforms. Great writers and musicians abound, and it's a minor golden age for the country.

Your onboard chronoskimmer's computer lets you know it has finished its calculations. It now displays the information you'll need to track down the thief — the people she may have met and the possible places she may have gone.

If you want to investigate:
Tchaikovsky — go to 60
Leo Tolstoy — go to 164
Anton Chekhov — go to 144

If you're ready to move to:
Germany in the year 1766 — go to 92
Germany in the year 1825 — go to 43
America in the year 1829 — go to 6

32. This is France in the year 1420, and it's in bad shape! The Hundred Years War with England (which actually lasted 116 years) is raging. Henry V of England has won the battle of Agincourt (1415) and is defeating the French soundly. But France isn't finished yet, and help is on the way for the Dauphin, the prince who

will some day be king.

Your chronoskimmer's computer tells you that it has calculated that the thief you're trailing talked to three people. The thief then moved on to one of three times and places.

If you want to question:
Joan of Arc — go to 145
Charles VII — go to 36
Henry V — go to 77

If you're ready to move to:
England in the year 1575 — go to 28
England in the year 1845 — go to 133
France in the year 1812 — go to 89

33. John Constable was one of England's greatest painters. Although he painted Salisbury Cathedral several times, Constable is best known for his landscapes. *The Haywain*, a picture of a cart carrying hay, is his most famous work. In his paintings, Constable loved to use shading to show the way light fell onto a scene, and when you find him, he's hard at work on another canvas. He takes a few minutes away from his work to talk to you about the thief you're after.

"Yes," he tells you, "I saw the thief you're trailing. He has brown eyes. Doesn't have any taste in art, though. I showed him what I was doing, and he said he preferred another painting. He called it *Impression: Sunrise* and said he was off to take a look at it next."

You tell Constable that you think his painting is very fine and head back to base (130) to check out this lead.

34. You land in America in the year 1780. The Revolutionary War is in its fourth year, and Charleston, South Carolina, has just fallen to the British Army. You're in the wrong place, though, and better head for 17 before you're captured by the British!

35. Barbarossa is the nickname given to Frederick I, king of Germany, who invaded and conquered Italy in 1154. You can see that he got the name Barbarossa, which means "red beard," because he has a huge, deep red-colored beard that shakes when he laughs. He's laughing when you ask about the thief you're chasing.

"Ah, that scoundrel!" he tells you. "The black-haired lady devil! She tried to steal some of my jewels, and I had her chased out of here as fast as lightning. She did mention something about seeing a scientist who worked with electricity. Whatever that is."

"Bottled lightning," you tell him.

"Ah, that I could find a use for!" he laughs.

You thank him for his help and head back to your Chronoskimmer (80) to check out these clues.

36. You find the Dauphin, the future Charles VII of France. However, right now he's hiding from the English troops, unsure about what to do. You know what you're doing, though, and ask him about the crook you're hunting.

"He was here," Charles tells you. "But he didn't stay long. He said he was going to see the *Marriage of Figaro*. Do you know who this Figaro is and who he's marrying?"

"It's an opera," you explain. "A very famous one."

"It can't be that famous," Charles sniffs. "I've never heard of it."

"That's because it hasn't been written yet," you tell him. To avoid explaining any more, you hurry back to base (32) to check out this clue.

37. You find Frederic Remington hard at work in his studio. One of the most famous American painters of the wild west, he also made a number of bronze statues of western themes. He spent a lot of time in the west, getting to know the subjects, and his works are very authentic. You

admire his latest painting and ask him about the crook you're after.

"He was here," Remington tells you. "The scoundrel tried to steal my latest bronze. I pulled my six-guns and sent him packing in a hurry!"

"Any idea where he might have gone?" you ask.

"Yes. I promised to blow him clear to China if he showed his face here again. Then he yelled back that, speaking of China, he was off to see Marco Polo. Strange fellow."

You agree with that and head back to your Chronoskimmer (106) to check out this new lead.

38. Madame Curie is hard at work in her laboratory when you arrive. She was born in Poland, but now works in Paris with her husband, Pierre. Together, they did early work in the field of radioactivity, and they discovered the element radium. One of the most famous scientists of all time, Madame Curie won two Nobel prizes for her work. When you arrive she takes a short break to answer your questions.

"Yes, the woman you are looking for was here," she tells you. "She seemed to be very nervous and said she had to go. It seems that she had an appointment to meet a Dutch painter. She wanted to have her picture painted."

Thanking her for her help, you head back to base (103) to check out this clue.

39. Alexandre Dumas turns out to be a quiet man, not at all like the heroic characters he has created in his famous books *The Three Musketeers* and *The Count of Monte Christo*. He greets you as you arrive and takes a break from his work. You ask him about the thief you're tracking.

"She stopped by and then hurried off," he tells you. "She told me that she had tickets for a performance of *Romeo And Juliet*."

You return to your Chronoskimmer (14) to try and figure things out.

40. You arrive at the country home of Charles Darwin. He's still working on the notes that he gathered during his trip around the world on the *HMS Beagle* . These notes will eventually lead to his famous theory of evolution. Right now, though, Darwin is not sure what to make of it all. He is checking out the differences in birds' beaks when he stops to talk with you.

"Why, yes," he tells you. "I've seen the man that you're looking for. In fact, he's in the other room right now. Come and see." He leads you to the library, but something makes you suspicious. You motion him aside and open the door just a tiny bit.

As you suspected, there's a string tied on the inside of the doorknob. If you were to open the door, the string would pull tight and light a stick of dynamite on the table! A sneaky little trap, if you weren't ready for it.

"Could I have a glass of water?" you ask Darwin.

"Thirsty work, eh?" he says as he gets it for you. But you don't drink it. Instead, you tell Darwin to pull the door open fast.

When he does, the dynamite lights. But you're ready, and before it can explode, you throw the water all over it, putting it out. This was a close call. It means you're not far from catching the crook — if you can live long enough to do it. It's time to return to base (133) and check out another of those leads.

41. Paul Revere is best known for the "midnight ride" he took during the Revolutionary War to warn people that "the British are coming!" But before the war — and after it, too — he was a noted silversmith and engraver. You find him working in his shop, and he puts down his tools to greet you. You ask him about the man you're after.

"Yes, he was in here," Revere tells you. "I caught him trying to steal some of my silver, and that's when I threw him out."

"Any idea where he might be headed?" you ask.

"Well, he did mention that he wanted to see *The Haywain*, a painting, I'm told."

Thanking him for his help, you head back to your Chronoskimmer (134) to record this clue.

42. In 1652, Jan van Rieebeck was sent by the Dutch East India Company to start a colony in South Africa. There he built a fort at Table Mountain and encouraged farmers to settle down. When you arrive he's organizing the colony, but he takes the time to answer your questions.

"Yes, I remember the woman you're looking for," he tells you. "She said she was going to look for Rip Van Winkle. I told her that we don't have anyone by that name here."

"I'm not surprised," you reply. "He's a fictional character."

"Ah! An alias!" van Rieebeck guesses. "I wonder what his real name is?"

Well, the story won't be written for another 140 years, so you can't blame him for being confused. You head back to your Chronoskimmer (18), hoping you don't get confused yourself!

43. You've reached Germany in the year 1825.

Actually, it's not the Germany of modern times, because several states, including Prussia, still are not a part of it. But many states have united in the wake of Napoleon's march across Europe, and the country is starting to take shape.

Also taking shape is the information from your chronoskimmer's computer. It tells you that your crook met three people and then went to one of three possible places and times.

If you want to talk to:

Richard Wagner — go to 120

Georg Hegel — go to 56

Ludwig von Beethoven — go to 168

If you're ready to move to:

America in the year 1861 — go to 27

America in the year 1960 — go to 96

France in the year 1921 — go to 160

44. Benedict Arnold is now living out the last few years of his life in London. Once considered a great man in the American cause for independence, he felt slighted by criticisms and plotted to betray the Americans to the British. Arnold's plans were discovered, and he had to flee for his life. Now the infamous traitor is in exile. You meet with him and ask about the crook you're hunting.

"Oh, he was here," Arnold tells you. "He said he admired me a lot and then asked for my autograph. As he was leaving, he mentioned that he was off to see a sculptor."

You head back to your Chronoskimmer (161) and check out this clue.

45. You're in Tin Pan Alley, the music publishing center of America. All the latest music is printed here, ready to be played all over the country. There're lots of hot hits, but a cold trail for you, since there's no sign of Nosmo King. Time to head to 54.

46. You've tracked Lady Agatha Wayland to one of the huge country manors that were built in England during this period. It seems like the right place to find her, but she's not here. Finally, realizing you've been had, you head for 54.

47. You arrive at a performance being given by Leonard Bernstein and the New York Philharmonic, the orchestra he conducted for many years. *West Side Story*, his famous musical, is being revived on Broadway. He's also appearing in television shows that explain music to young people. In addition, he has written a book. It seems like this is Bernstein's year.

You are beginning to wonder if it's your year, though. Listening to Bernstein conduct, you almost miss seeing the thug who slips next to you. He's about to draw his gun when you spot him. Quickly, you give him a karate chop to the neck, and he collapses.

The people in front of you at the concert turn around and tell you to keep quiet.

You are just about to answer them when you spot a piece of paper tucked into the thugs concert program. Pulling it out, you give a whoop of joy. It's a list of addresses for Carmen's gang! The people in front of you turn around again.

"Either shut up or leave," they hiss.

"Just going," you tell them as you handcuff the thief to his theater chair and go in search of possible suspects.

If you think the suspect is:
Pete Moss — go to 68
Sybil Servant — go to 10
Carmen Sandiego — go to 124
Scar Greynolt — go to 108
Lady Agatha Wayland — go to 51
Fast Eddie B — go to 152
Heidi Gosikh — go to 84
Nosmo King — go to 23

48. Hereward the Wake turns out to be an Englishman who fought against the Norman con-

querors. He and his men hid in the marshy land called the Fens, just outside of the town of Ely. More like robbers than freedom fighters, Hereward and his followers sometimes attacked their own people when they needed food or supplies for themselves. You manage to find Hereward's camp, and you ask about the thief you're track.

"He was here," Hereward replies. "A funny sort of fellow. He wanted me to sign an autograph for him, but he seemed very upset when I told him I never learned to read or write. He had me carve a notch into the handle of his gun instead."

"Any idea where he might have gone?" you ask.

"Well," he replies, "he did mention that where he was going he could take a trip abroad to meet a famous traitor."

You head back to your Chronoskimmer (105) to work on this new lead.

49. Emile Zola turns out to be a writer, who's finishing his most famous book, *Nana*. But Zola will become best known for championing the cause of a soldier named Dreyfus in 1898. Dreyfus was sent to Devil's Island for a crime he didn't commit, and it was mainly Zola's refusal to allow this terrible abuse of justice that set the man free.

Right now, Zola lays aside his pen and greets you politely. You ask if he's seen the thief you're chasing.

"He passed by here," he tells you. "He mentioned that on his next voyage he was going to see a soldier in America."

You thank him for his help and return to base (58) to check out this clue.

50. Sir H. Rider Haggard is a big, bearded man, who, although very interested in farming, is

making his living as a writer of adventure stories. The two best known stories are *King Solomon's Mines* and *She*. Both of these tales are set in Africa, where Haggard spent many of his early years. He greets you cheerfully as you arrive, and you ask about the crook you're looking for.

"Yes, I saw her," he tells you. "Red-haired woman. Tried to tell me how to milk my cows! What a nerve! I told her to clear off and bother somebody else, and she said she was just heading off to get an autograph of someone by the name of Mucha."

You wish him well with his books and head back to the Chromoskimmer (127) to check out these clues.

51. You've trailed Lady Agatha Wayland to Hollywood in 1960. The top-rated show on TV this year is "Gunsmoke," and you think she might be after Dennis Weaver's autograph (he plays the very popular deputy Chester Goode on the show). But the lead turns out to be a dead-end, and you have to take a trip to 54.

52. Lucretia Borgia is a member of a large and very powerful Italian family that is noted for the ruthless treatment it deals out to anyone who gets in its way. Actually, you find Lucretia is not as bad as you've heard. It seems she's an art

lover. On the other hand, remembering that she is most famous for poisoning people, you decide not to have a drink with her! Instead, you ask about the villain you're after.

"He was here a while ago," she tells you. "He wanted to take me to dinner, but I refused. You never know what might be in your food, do you? Would you like a piece of chicken?"

You thank her kindly but tell her you just ate. "Any idea where he might have gone?"

"He was very upset when I wouldn't go on a date with him, so he said he was going to a date where he could meet a queen. I told him he'd better be careful not to lose his head when he meets her, or he might really lose his head!"

You beat a quick retreat before she can offer you anything else to eat or drink. You head off to the Chronoskimmer (69) to check out this new information.

53. You're in America in the year 1910. This is the year the Boy Scouts of America was founded. And, speaking of found, you've found this is the wrong place to be. Time to head for 17.

54. Well, you've managed to make it to the right place and time, but you've taken out an arrest warrant for the wrong person, so the crook

has escaped with the loot. For that mistake, add ten points onto your travel points and then go to the back of the book and see how you've done. Better be a bit more careful next time.

55. You're in Holland in the year 1660. As in most of Europe, Holland is overflowing with talent in many fields — science, art, literature, and exploration to name a few. This is an exciting time and an exciting country. It's a shame you have to be here just to work, but those are the breaks.

You hear a buzz. It's the chronoskimmer's computer telling you that it has finished analyzing the energy fields. It prints out a list of three people the thief met and three possible places the crook could have gone.

If you want to investigate:
Rembrandt — go to 147
Christiaan Huygens — go to 95
Spinoza — go to 111

If you're moving to:
England in the year 1718 — go to 9
France in the year 1701 — go to 63
England in the year 1650 — go to 131

56. You arrive at the University of Berlin,

where Hegel is giving one of his famous lectures. You listen and try to understand, but it doesn't make a whole lot of sense to you. Something about ideas and their opposites. You almost ask him what the opposite of an idea could be, but then you get an idea of your own — you'll only ask him about the thief you're after. You just hope he'll speak in simple language!

"Yes, I saw the woman you seek," he tells you. "She wanted my autograph. Most flattering. She didn't stay very long, though. She said she had an appointment to meet a president."

You thank him for his help — and for using words you could understand! — and head back to your Chronoskimmer (43) to check out this clue.

57. You're arrived in America in 1900. This is the year when Carrie Nation, a woman crusading against the use of alcohol, began to visit bars, which she smashed up with a hatchet! You might as well be with her, for all the good you're doing here, but you move along to 17 instead.

58. This is France, and the year is 1880. It's busy time of change. The workplace is changing from farmlands to work in cities. France and other European countries are dividing up Africa among themselves. In the cities, many modern conve-

niences, such as lighting and sewers, are becoming common.

Your chronoskimmer's computer starts to buzz to let you know it's finished analyzing the energy fields. It has tracked the thief to three different people and has discovered three possible places the crook might have gone. Let's hope the people here can help you narrow those three places down to one!

If you want to talk to:
Jacques Offenbach — *go to 90*
Emile Zola — *go to 49*
Claude Monet — *go to 150*

If you think the thief went to:
America in the year 1521 — *go to 12*
America in the year 1875 — *go to 106*
America in the year 1925 — *go to 74*

59. You've trailed Heidi Gosikh to London. It's a busy, messy city, filled with twisting roads, bad drains, and some very suspicious-looking characters. Unfortunately, none of them looks like Heidi, so you'd better go to 54.

60. When you arrive at Tchaikovsky's house, you find him playing the piano. Tchaikovsky is famous for works such as the 1st Piano ☞

Concerto, as well as for his ballet *Swan Lake*. Right now, he's working on his Symphony No. 6, the *Pathetique*, but he takes a break to talk to you. You ask him about the crook you're chasing.

"She stopped to visit me," he tells you. "Said she always wanted to be a ballerina, but she dances very badly, and I had to tell her so. She got all offended and said she was going to talk to a German composer about getting a part in one of his operas. I just hope she sings better than she dances."

"I doubt it," you tell him. "She's got a voice that breaks glass. It probably helps her in her robberies." You thank him for his help and head back to base (31) to check out what you've learned.

61. You've arrived in Spain in the year 1502. Columbus has just set off on his fourth (and last) trip to America, and the forces of Spain are all set to conquer the continent in search of the gold and spices they think are there. One man, Ponce de Leon, will hunt for a Fountain of Youth there!

The chronoskimmer's computer beeps to let you know it's finished checking the energy readings. It seems that the thief had time to talk to three people. The crook then fled to one of three times and places.

If you want to interrogate:

Hernan Cortes — go to 65
Queen Isabella — go to 121
Francisco Pizarro — go to 109

If you've tracked the crook to:
China in the year 1200 — go to 24
France in the year 1420 — go to 32
France in the year 1672 — go to 81

62. John Hancock was born wealthy and used a lot of his money to support the new United States during the Revolutionary War. He was the first person to sign the Declaration of Independence (which is why to this day someone's signature is called his or her "John Hancock") and was the first Governor of Massachusetts. All of that is still in his future though, for it is only 1752 and Hancock is just nineteen years old. You greet him and ask about the robber you're hunting.

"Aye, I saw the villain," Hancock tells you. "I just wish I could have stopped him from taking the Liberty Bell. But I did overhear him say he wanted to go for a ride in a very early steam locomotive — I didn't have a clue what he meant."

But you do and you thank him for his help and head back to your Chronoskimmer (134) to check on this information.

63. You've arrived in France in the year 1701. It's a time known as "The Enlightenment," because it was during this time that philosophers began to explore how humans think and function in the world around them. France was one of the leaders in philosophy at this time, but you're not thinking clearly — you shouldn't even be here. Better head straight to 17.

64. This is Italy, and the year is 1182. The country is split into many tiny city-states, which quarrel among themselves to see which is the strongest. There's no sign of the thief here, and you give up and head for 17.

65. You find seventeen-year-old Hernan Cortes practicing his swordfighting. You try to get his attention.

"Just a few more strokes," he promises. "I'm going to Hispaniola in America in a couple of years, and I want to be in top form!"

As he swings away, you can see why one day he will become a famous soldier who will destroy the empire of the Aztecs under its great leader, Montezuma. But that won't be for another than ten years. Finally, he stops and listens to your questions.

"The thief you seek was here," he tells you.

"He said I was too young to be a great soldier, but what does he know? All great men are young at one time. He said he was going to a place where where he could meet a real soldier."

You wish him well with his practice and return to your base (61) to check out this clue.

66. You've landed in Italy in the year 1269. Marco Polo will soon be leaving Venice to head to China. You'd better be leaving, too, but not for China. Go to 17.

67. You're in America in 1937. Amelia Earhart, the well-known pilot, has been lost at sea. You're lost at sea too, because the thief you're after isn't here. Time to go to 17.

68. You reach Cape Canaveral, where the first weather satellite is about to go into orbit to help with weather forecasting. It might as well be raining, because there's no sign of Pete Moss here. Finally, you give up and head to 54.

69. You're in Italy in the year 1514, a time of great learning and brilliant people. This period in history is known as the Renaissance, meaning "rebirth," because so many ideas were born or rediscovered. Many scientists, scholars, and artists who will be

famous throughout the centuries are presently at work. If you had the time, you would like to visit some of them. Unfortunately, your job comes first.

The chronoskimmer's computer finishes its scan of the energy patterns and tells you that the crook you're looking for spoke to three people and went to one of three possible times and places.

If you want to check out:
Michaelangelo — go to 101
Lucretia Borgia — go to 52
Leonardo da Vinci — go to 7

If you want to investigate:
Spain in the year 1502 — go to 61
America in the year 1525 — go to 125
England in the year 1875 — go to 169

70. You've tracked Heidi Gosikh to a dance parlor. In places like this, the fashionable flapper girls of the Twenties led dancing marathons, some of which lasted for an entire week. But Heidi isn't here. Time to head for 54.

71. You're in America in 1850. The United States is growing — just this year California became the thirty-first state! Gold fever is catching on all over the country, as news of the big strike in California has everyone all fired up. But you don't have the time to

go hunting for gold — you're hunting for a crook.

The chronoskimmer's computer has finished its work and gives you the results. The villain you're seeking met with three people and then left for one of three possible times and places. With luck, you'll be able to narrow things down.

If you want to talk to:

Abraham Lincoln — go to 83

Mark Twain — go to 5

Jesse James — go to 135

If you're ready to move on, for:

England in the year 1547 — go to 159

Spain in the year 1478 — go to 30

England in the year 1885 — go to 127

72. You're reached France, and the year is 1850. This is a time of social struggle, with unhappy crowds rebelling against the government. It's not a good time for you to be here, and you discover that the thief you're after isn't here either. Time to move on to 17.

73. You've tracked Pete Moss to a country house, where the owners are having high tea in their garden. They invite you to join them, but you have to say no. It's obvious that Moss has slipped away, so you head for 54.

74. You arrive in America in the year 1925. The composer George Gershwin is very popular this year, and his "Rhapsody In Blue" is a big hit. Sadly, the thief you're tracking isn't here. Better head for 17.

75. You've tracked Scar Graynolt to a wig shop in London. George I is king of England, and wigs are all the rage — for men! You wonder if Scar has tried to disguise himself. If he has, then he's been so successful even you can't find him. Finally, you give up and head for 54.

76. When you finally reach Napoleon, you're amazed to see that he's quite a short man — not much over five feet tall. Now that he's conquered a good deal of Europe, he has a lot on his mind. Napoleon won't be defeated until he invades Russia (in 1812) and then meets General Wellington at Waterloo (in 1815). Right now, though, he's on top of the world.

"I'm a busy man," he snaps at you. "What do you want?" You ask him about the villain you're chasing, and he frowns. "Yes, she came here. I threw her out for wasting my time. She yelled something about going to see a queen with better manners than mine." He looks at you. "Now, are you going, or shall I throw you out, too?"

You leave quickly and head back to your Chronoskimmer (14) to check out this lead!

77. Since you're in France, you're rather surprised to find that Henry V, king of France, is English! He's examining papers and signing them, with all of his lords and generals around him. When you ask one of the lords to clear things up for you, he explains that Henry defeated the French at Agincourt five years ago and was then declared heir to the French throne. You know that this arrangement won't last long, however, thanks to people like Joan of Arc. For the moment, though, the English rule France.

Henry finishes his paperwork and then agrees to see you. You ask about the crook you're hunting, and Henry nods.

"He was here," he tells you. "He did say something about wanting to read a book called *Robinson Crusoe*. Sounds daft to me, but there you are."

You return to the Chronoskimmer (32) to check out this clue.

78. You find Marco Polo in charge of one of the Chinese provinces. China has been ruled for many years by Kublai Khan, and he likes this young Italian. As a result, he keeps Marco working for him. Marco is busy learning everything

he can about the Yangchow province.

"I aim to write a book about all of my adventures when I return home to Venice," Marco tells you. "I've taken plenty of notes, you know."

You tell him he's doing a great job. His book will later inspire people like Christopher Columbus to go off in search of new lands. Right now, though, you ask Marco about the crook you're chasing.

"He was here," Marco tells you, studying his notes. "He mentioned that he wanted to meet a flying man. Now, I've seen many strange things in this country, but I've never seen a man who could fly."

"That won't happen for many years yet," you tell Marco to get him to stop worrying that he's missed something interesting. Then you head back to base (162) to check out this clue.

79. When you arrive at the home of Maurice Ravel, you hear piano music coming from inside. Ravel composed most of his music for the piano, which was his favorite instrument, but he is best known for his lovely *Bolero*, which repeats the same tune on different instruments of the orchestra.

He stops playing to talk to you, and you ask about the robber you're after.

"She stopped by a while ago," he tells you. "She

couldn't stay long, though, because she said she had to see two people. First she was going to meet a painter in his native country, and then she was taking a quick trip to get Galileo's autograph."

You thank Ravel for his help and leave him to his music as you head back to the Chronoskimmer (103) to check out this new clue.

80. Italy in the year 1174 is made up of a lot of small city-states that disagree with one another. The German king, Frederick I, has conquered a number of them, forcing them together for the first time. It's a time of change and unrest, and you hope you won't be here very long.

The chronoskimmer's computer that's built into your Chronoskimmer beeps to let you know it's finished checking the energy patterns in the air. You read the results. According to the chronoskimmer's computer, the thief met with three people and then left. The chronoskimmer's computer can't pinpoint where the crook went, but it's one of three times and places. You just hope that one of the people the villain spoke to can help you track down the crook.

If you want to talk to:
Barbarossa — go to 35
Alexander III — go to 104
Bonanno Pisano — go to 148

Sybil Servant

Sex: Female
Hair: Red
Eyes: Grey
Occupation: Retired Government clerk.
Favorite Food: East Indian
Weakness: Too bossy!

Carmen Sandiego

Sex: Female
Hair: Brown
Eyes: Brown
Occupation: Former Spy for the Intelligence Service of Monaco.
Favorite Food: Mexican
Weakness: Too smart for her own good.

Heidi Gosikh

Sex: Female
Hair: Black
Eyes: Brown
Occupation: Mechanic
Favorite Food: Southern
Weakness: Loves loud music so much that police find her during a crime.

Lady Agatha Wayland

Sex: Female
Hair: Red
Eyes: Green
Occupation: Reads mystery stories.
Favorite Food: Mexican
Weakness: A terrible driver sometimes has an accident before a crime.

Carmen Sandiego

Sybil Servant

Lady Agatha Wayland

Heidi Gosikh

Pete Moss

Scar Graynolt

Fast Eddie B.

Nosmo King

Scar Graynolt

Sex: Male
Hair: Red
Eyes: Hazel
Occupation: Street Musician
Favorite Food: Spanish
Weakness: So relaxed he sometimes oversleeps and misses the crime.

Pete Moss

Sex: Male
Hair: Black
Eyes: Brown
Occupation: Gardener
Favorite Food: Fresh fruit
Weakness: He can't resist digging in a garden, even if he is on the job with Carmen. If he sees a weed, he gets down on his knees and starts pulling!

Nosmo King

Sex: Male
Hair: Brown
Eyes: Hazel
Occupation:
Favorite Food: Scottish
Weakness: Hopeless jerk. Always flirting with the ladies but never sucessful.

Fast Eddie B.

Sex: Male
Hair: Black
Eyes: Brown
Occupation: Professional Croquet Player
Favorite Food: Japanese
Weakness: Plans crimes so complex they never work out.

THE LAST DODO BIRD

Location: Mauritus, 1681
Background: A turkey-sized bird that couldn't fly, the Dodo is now known for its stupidity. the birds would simply stand about and allow sailors to kill them for food. "As dead as a Dodo" became a well-know phrase.

To investigate this crime:
Go to 18

THE LEANING TOWER OF PISA

Location: Pisa, Italy, 1174 AD
Background: The tower is a bell tower of white marble, supposedly built by Bonanno Pisano in 1174, but not finished for 200 years. The foundations were unsound and it began to tilt over from the very beginning. Despite this, it is now 184 feet tall, and leans a total of 17 feet from its base.

To investigate this crime:
Go to 80

THE CROWN JEWELS

Location: The Tower of London, England 1066 A.D.
Background: The Crown Jewels are the most famous treasuries in England. They are the traditional jewels worn when a King or Queen is crowned. Most famous is St. Edward's Crown, originally made for Edward the Confessor in 1066. This and the other jewels are on display in Tower of London.

To investigate this crime:
Go to 105

THE LIBERTY BELL

Location: Philadelphia, America 1752 AD
Background: The Liberty Bell was made in London and shipped to America in 1752. It rang on many historic occasions, including the official announcement of the Declaration of Independence on July 8, 1776.

To investigate this crime: Go to 134

THE LEANING TOWER
OF PISA

THE LAST DODO BIRD

THE LIBERTY BELL

THE CROWN JEWELS

Writers

Artists

Musicians

Explorers

ARTISTS

1. Leonardo da Vinci (1452–1519). Italian painter and inventor who painted the *Mona Lisa* in 1504.
2. Michaelanglo (1475–1564). Italian painter and sculptor who finished the statue *David* between 1501–1504.
3) Rembrandt van Rijn (1606–1669). Dutch painter who finished *The Night Watch* in 1642.
4. Joseph Turner (1775–1851). English painter who finished *Frosty Morning* in 1813.
5. John Constable (1776–1837). English painter who finished *The Haywain* in 1821.
6. Claude Monet (1840–1926). French painter who finished *Impression: Sunrise* in 1874.
7. Vincent Van Gogh (1853–1890). Dutch painter who finished *The Starry Night* in 1889.
8. Alphonse Mucha (1860–1939). French designer who painted *The Seasons* in 1896.
9. Frederic Remington (1861–1909). American sculptor who painted *Cavalry Charge on the Southern Plains* in 1907.
10) Pablo Picasso (1881–1973). Spanish painter who completed the painting *Guernica* in 1937.

WRITERS

1. Dante Alighieri (1265–1321). Italian poet, who wrote *The Divine Comedy* in 1321.
2. Sir Thomas More (1478–1535). English author who wrote *Utopia* in 1516.
3. William Shakespeare (1564–1616). English playwright who wrote *Romeo and Juliet* in 1595.
4. Daniel Defoe (1660–1731). English author who wrote *Robinson Crusoe* in 1719.
5. Washington Irving (1783–1859). American author who wrote *Rip Van Winkle* in 1820.
6. Alexandre Dumas (1802–1870). French author who wrote *The Three Musketeers* in 1844.
7. Mark Twain also known as Samuel Clements (1835–1910). American author who wrote *Huckleberry Finn* in 1884.
8. Sir H. Rider Haggard (1856–1925). English author who wrote *King Solomon's Mines* in 1885.
9. Anton Chekhov (1856–1904). Russian playwright who wrote *Uncle Vanya* in 1897.
10) Rudyard Kipling (1865–1936). English author who wrote *The Jungle Book* in 1894.

EXPLORERS

1). Erik The Red (10th century). Icelandic discoverer of Greenland, and America (985).
2. Marco Polo (1254–1324). Italian traveler to China (1271–1295).
3. Christopher Columbus (1451–1506). Italian sailor who discovered America (1492. for Spain.
4. Francisco Pizarro (1474–1541). Spanish soldier who invaded Peru between 1526–1527.
5. Ferdinand Magellan (1480–1521). Portuguese sailor who traveled around the world.
6. Sir Francis Drake (1543–1596). English sailor who went around the world (1577–80).
7. Captain James Cook (1728–1779). English explorer of Australia and New Zealand between 1768–1771).
8. David Livingstone (1813–1873). English missionary to Africa (from 1841).
9. Admiral Richard Byrd (1888–1957). American airman who flew over South Pole in 1929.
10. Neil Armstrong (born 1930). American astronaut who was the first man to walk on the Moon (1969).

MUSICIANS

1. Antonio Vivaldi (1669–1741). Italian composer of *The Four Seasons* in 1725.
2. Wolfgang Amedeus Mozart (1756–1791). German composer who wrote *The Marriage of Figaro* in 1786.
3) Ludwig Von Beethoven (1770–1827). German composer who wrote *Symphony #9 (Ode to Joy.* in 1824.
4. Richard Wagner (1813–1883). German composer who wrote *The Ride of the Valkyries* in 1852.
5. Jacques Offenbach (1819–1880). French composer who wrote *Orpheus In The Underworld* in 1858.
6. Johann Strauss II (1825–1899). Austrian composer who wrote *The Blue Danube Waltz* in 1867.
7. Peter Tchaikovsky (1840–1893). Russian composer wrote *The Nutcracker Suite* in 1891.
8. Sir Arthur Sullivan (1842–1900). English composer who wrote *The Pirates of Penzance* in 1879 with another composer W. S. Gilbert.
9. Maurice Ravel (1875–1937). French composer who wrote *Bolero* in 1928.
10. Leonard Bernstein (1918–1990). American composer who wrote *West Side Story* in 1957.

RULERS

1. Richard I "The Lionheart" (1157–1199). Ruled England between 1188–1199.
2. Henry V (1387–1422). Ruled France between 1413–1422.
3. Charles VII (1403–1461). Ruled France between 1422–1461.
4. Ferdinand (1452–1516) and Isabella (1451–1504). Ruled Spain between 1474–1516.
5. Elizabeth I (1533–1603). Ruled England between 1558–1603.
6. Louis XIV "The Sun King" (1638–1715). Ruled France between 1643–1715.
7. George Washington (1732–1799). President of the United States between 1789–1797.
8. Abraham Lincoln (1809–1865). President of the United States between 1860–1865.
9. Queen Victoria (1819–1901). Ruled England between 1837–1901.
10. John F. Kennedy (1917–1963). President of the United States between 1960–1963.

SCIENTISTS

1. Nicolaus Copernicus (1473–1543). Polish astronomer who proved Earth goes round the sun.
2. Galileo Galilei (1564–1642). Italian scientist who used telescope to discover craters on the Moon.
3. Sir Isaac Newton (1642–1726). English scientist who explained gravity and motion (1684).
4. Alessandro Volta (1745–1827). French inventor of the first battery (1800).
5. George Stephenson (1781–1848). English builder of locomotives (1814).
6. Charles Darwin (1809–1882). English naturalist who formulated a theory of evolution (1859).
7. Thomas Alva Edison (1847–1931). American inventor of the light bulb (1879).
8. Marie Curie (1867–1934). Polish-French discoverer of radioactivity (1898).
9. Wilbur (1867–1912) and Orville Wright (1871–1948). Americans who built the first airplane (1903).
10. Albert Einstein (1879–1945). Swiss-American discoverer of The Theory of Relativity (1905).

SOLDIERS

1. El Cid [Rodrigo Diaz de Vivar] (1043–1099). Spanish soldier who fought for independence.
2. Saladin [Salah ad-Din] (1138–1193). Arabic soldier in the Middle East.
3. Genghis Khan (1167–1227). Mogol conqueror of China.
4. Joan of Arc (1412–1431). French freedom fighter and saint.
5. Herman Cortes (1485–1547). Spanish conqueror of the Aztecs of America.
6. Napoleon Bonaparte (1769–1821). French invader of Europe, Russia, and Egypt.
7. Duke of Wellington (1769–1852). English General who defeated Napoleon.
8. Robert E. Lee (1807–1870). Confederate General in the Civil War.
9. Sitting Bull (1831–1890). Native American defeated General Custer at the Battle of Little Big Horn.
10. General George Patton (1885–1945). American soldier in Africa and Europe.

CRIMINALS

1. Thomas de Torquemada (1420–1498). Spanish leader of the Inquisition.
2. Lucretia Borgia (1480–1519). Member of famous Italian family who was suspected of poisoning people.
3. Ivan the Terrible (1530–1584). Russian ruler and tyrant.
4. Henry Morgan (1635–1688). English pirate and destroyer of Panama City.
5. Blackbeard [Edward Teach] (died 1718). English pirate who terrorized the West Indian Seas.
6. Benedict Arnold (1741–1801). An American traitor during the revolutionary War.
7. Maximilien Robespiere (1758–1794). French ruler who began the "Reign of Terror."
8. John Wilkes Booth (1838–1865). An American actor and assassin of President Lincoln.
9. Jesse James (1847–1882). An American train and bank robber.
10. Al Capone (1899–1947). An American gangster.

Scientists

Rulers

Criminals

Soldiers

SCORE CARD 1

Stolen Object:_____

Clues: _____

_____
_____
_____
_____

**Suspect
to arrest:**_____

Move points

Total Move points: _____

Total Game Score: _____

SCORE CARD 2

Stolen Object:_____

Clues: _____

_____
_____
_____
_____

**Suspect
to arrest:**_____

Move points

Total Move points: _____

Total Game Score: _____

SCORE CARD 3

Stolen Object:_____

Clues: _____

_____
_____
_____
_____

**Suspect
to arrest:**_____

Move points

Total Move points: _____

Total Game Score: _____

SCORE CARD 4

Stolen Object:_____

Clues: _____

_____
_____
_____
_____

**Suspect
to arrest:**_____

Move points

Total Move points: _____

Total Game Score: _____

If you think the thief went to:
France in the year 1807 — go to 14
America in the year 1892 — go to 128
France in the year 1850 — go to 72

81. You arrive in France in the year 1672. It's the reign of Louis XIV, who is known as "The Sun King" because of his wealth and influence. There's no sign of the crook you're after. Time to go to 17.

82. You arrive in Menlo Park, where Thomas Alva Edison has his inventor's shop. Edison was a genius in many ways, having made over a thousand inventions in his life. Right now, he's working on improving the telephone. Soon he will invent the phonograph, the electric lightbulb, and the first motion-picture camera. Edison is a very cheery and chatty man, who is most happy to stop his work to talk to you.

"Yes, I saw that black-haired scoundrel you're looking for," he tells you. "I suspected he was looking for something to steal, so I threw him out. I heard him say he wanted to read something Dante wrote, but it wasn't *The Divine Comedy*. He said that where he was going, that work wasn't written yet.

You thank Edison for his help and head off to base (106) to check out these leads.

83. One day, Abraham Lincoln will become one of the greatest presidents in American history. Right now, though, in the year 1850, his political career doesn't look too good. He used to be in the House of Representatives, but last year, when he opposed the American war with Mexico, he lost his seat. He invites you into his house in a kindly manner.

"Take a seat," he insists as he calls for afternoon tea for you. "How can I help you?"

You ask him about the thief you're tracking, and he rubs his beard.

"The lady you seek was certainly here," he recalls. "I remember her saying that she had to read Utopia." He gestures to his bookcase, filled with law books. "I apologized for not having a copy that I could lend her, but she said she would be able to get one at her next stop."

You thank him for the help and for the delicious tea. You head back to your Chronoskimmer (71) to follow up on this information.

84. You've tracked Heidi Gosikh into the Greenwich Village section of New York City. Right now, a new form of art is being developed here. One of the leaders of this new type of art, which will be called "Pop Art," is Andy Warhol. A lot of would-be artists live in the Greenwich Village

area, and you see many examples of the new style. Some look like piles of junk sprayed with paint. Others seem to be all curves, loops, and lines. None of them looks much like art to you.

Then you spot Heidi, sneaking into Warhol's house. Definitely up to no good! You wait outside, hiding, until she comes out. She's carrying a piece of artwork that looks like a big block of stone with holes shot through it.

Quickly, you grab the artwork from her and then push it down over her head. She fits right into one of the holes, which pins her arms to her side so she can't move.

You laugh. "Now, that's a picture I can admire," you tell her. "Let's get you down to the police station, where they'll take a few pictures of their own — for the rogues' gallery, not the art gallery, though!"

You find where Heidi's hidden the Leaning Tower of Pisa and arrange to have it returned to its proper place and time. Then you call the Chief to tell him the good news.

"I knew you could do it," he says. "Well done! Now why don't you go to the back of the book to see if you've earned a promotion?"

85. You've trailed Scar Graynolt to the Liverpool docks. Many of the ships carrying people to

America leave from here, and you wonder if Scar himself is trying to escape. But nobody here has seen him, and finally you give up and go to 54.

86. You arrive in Philadelphia, at the small shop run by Benjamin Franklin. An active and brilliant man, Franklin has been a printer, a writer, a philosopher, and a scientist. Already he has invented the bifocal glasses he wears and an efficient stove heater. One day, he will help write the Declaration of Independence, serve as assistant postmaster general, and be an ambassador to France. Right now, though, he's getting ready to fly a kite. Seeing your puzzled look, he laughs.

"No, I'm not being childish," he says. "I have this theory that lightning is actually made of electricity, and I need to test the theory by flying my kite in a storm until lightning hits it."

It sounds pretty dangerous to you, and not something you'd want to try. You ask him about the thief you're after while he's still in one piece.

"Yes, he was here. He wanted to know if I had a copy of *Rip Van Winkle*. To be honest, I had to admit I'd never heard of the story. Then he told me it hasn't been printed yet, and he'd have to go to a time after it had been written." Franklin smiles. "I suspect the man was not entirely all there."

"Maybe he'd been struck by lightning," you

suggest as you head back to your Chronoskimmer (134) to check out this clue.

87. You've arrived in Holland in the year 1870. It's a very pretty country that is beginning to look much as it does in the present. But there's no sign of the crook you're after, so you have to go to 17.

88. You're in the London theater district, where William Shakespeare has moved from being an actor to being a popular playwright. When you arrive, he's directing a rehearsal of his latest play, *Romeo And Juliet*. Shakespeare tells the actors to take a break so that he can talk to you. You notice that there are no women in the play, and that even Juliet is played by a man wearing a dress! But it's 1595, women aren't supposed to degrade themselves by acting. Although it seems pretty silly to you, you don't mention it. Instead, you ask Shakespeare about the thief you're hunting.

"Indeed," he replies, "I have seen the woman you seek. She asked me if she might play Juliet, and I told her that for a woman to act upon a public stage would be scandalous. She became offended and vowed to find a more enlightened playwright."

His lengthy words are making your head spin, so you thank him kindly for his help and leave in a hurry. Back to the Chronoskimmer (116) to check out this new lead!

89. You're in France, and the year is 1812. The mood here isn't good. For years now, Napoleon has been leading France from victory to victory all through Europe. But this year, he has made a terrible error; he attacked Russia. His army was beaten back, not by the Russians but by the weather. Napoleon is not the only loser right now — so are you. You're in the wrong place and had better move on to 17.

90. Jacques Offenbach is one of the most popular composers at this time in France. He has written *Orpheus in the Underworld*, a comic opera that was a failure until a newspaper reviewed it and said it was offensive and rude. Then everyone wanted to see it! After that he wrote *La Belle Helene*, and is now hard at work on a serious opera, *The Tales of Hoffman*. Offenbach puts down his pen to talk to you.

"Yes, I remember the man you're looking for," he tells you. "He told me he loved the can-can dance I wrote for Orpheus and wanted to hear it. I apologized and explained that I was working on a new piece. He certainly was annoyed at that. As he left, he said he was going to another time in which he could hear the music."

You leave and head back to base (58) to check out this new clue.

91. You arrive on the pirate ship that's carrying Edward Teach — better known as the horrible pirate Blackbeard. He's a huge man, and his long, thick, beard is curled. He's also a terrible man — and almost certain to be caught and punished for his crimes.

Quietly, you sneak up on him and use a karate chop to his neck to knock him out.

Maybe there's a clue hidden away somewhere? You creep down to Blackbeard's cabin and peer inside. There's a desk with something on it. You pick the something up and grin. It's a list of where Carmen's gang is hiding! Now you can catch the thief you're after!

If you think it's:

Carmen Sandiego — go to 167
Fast Eddie B — go to 26
Heidi Gosikh — go to 59
Pete Moss — go to 163
Sybil Servant — go to 115
Scar Graynolt — go to 75
Nosmo King — go to 99
Lady Agatha Wayland — go to 46

92. You've arrived in Germany in the year 1766. Actually, you're in Prussia, ruled by Frederick II.

During his reign, Prussia took over several neighboring states and formed the basis for modern Germany. You're in something of a state yourself — there's no sign of the thief you're trailing. You have to go straight to 17.

93. You arrive at the home of George Washington, in Mount Vernon, not far from Washington, D.C. In his lifetime, Washington was both the General of the Army that defeated the British in the Revolutionary War and also the first president of the newly formed United States of America. He refused to serve a third term as president, though, and has gone back to the quiet of the home he loves. Here you find him, relaxing on the porch. You ask him about the thief you're chasing.

"The man you seek was here," Washington replies. "He was admiring some of the paintings I have hanging in my house. But I suspected he was going to steal one, and so I sent him packing. He did say that he was going to take a look at the Mona Lisa next."

You thank him for his help and hurry back to base (161) to check out this lead.

94. You've traced Scar Graynolt to Roosevelt Field, the small airport where Charles Lindbergh took off for his nonstop flight to France just three

years ago. Maybe Graynolt is trying to hop on a plane to get away? But when you look around, nobody is here. After a while, you head to 54.

95. You reach the home of Christiaan Huygens, a noted Dutch scientist. Huygens studied light, improved clocks by adding a pendulum to them, and dabbled in astronomy. He discovered the rings around Saturn and the markings on Mars that would later be called canals. He puts aside the pages of calculations he's working on to greet you. You ask him about the crook you're chasing.

"She did stop by here," he tells you. "She had the most piercing gray eyes I've ever seen. Seemed quite keen on science, too. After we talked about my theories on light, she told me she was off to talk to Newton about his theory of gravity."

Thanking him for his help, you hurry back to your Chronoskimmer (55) to check up on these fresh leads.

96. You've arrived in America in 1960. It's the time of the young — in music, in art, and in films. The United States has its youngest-ever president in John Fitzgerald Kennedy. Rock 'n' roll swells to huge record sales.

Your chronoskimmer's computer beeps to let you know it's finished checking out the energy levels. It can find no trace of the thief having left this time and place and just three people the crook went to see.

If you want to check out:

Leonard Bernstein — go to 47
Neil Armstrong — go to 136
President Kennedy — go to 100

97. Edward the Confessor was King of England from 1042 to the year you are now in, 1066. He earned his name because he was a deeply religious man. Although he will promise the throne to William of Normandy, on his deathbed he will change his mind and appoint Harold king instead. This will lead up to William's famous invasion of England. As you arrive, Edward isn't too well, but he agrees to a short chat with you. You ask him about the thief you're hunting.

"A brown-eyed man?" he says. "He was here. He stole the crown I had made for myself, as well as the rest of the jewels. One of my guards heard him say he was off to see a president — whatever one of those is."

"It's the ruler of America," you explain. "He's elected into office by the people."

Edward looks puzzled. "Sounds silly to me. You'd be much better off with a king." Knowing what this king is going to do to England, you

58

doubt it, but you don't tell him that. Instead, you head back to your Chronoskimmer (105) to enter this new information.

98. You've arrived in America in the year 1930. Last year, Wall Street stocks collapsed, and the country is just entering the Great Depression. People will starve, many will lose their homes, and crime is raging in many cities. Gangsters fight it out and smuggle illegal whiskey and beer all over the country. Yet, despite all of the problems, people still seem to have fun. New dances sweep the country, and movie houses are more popular than ever. Talking pictures are finally here, and there's talk that almost any year now they'll be able to make movies in color, too!

The chronoskimmer's computer finishes checking the energy levels and tells you that the thief is definitely here, somewhere. The crook's met with three people, so maybe one of them can help you.

If you want to see:
Admiral Byrd — go to 170
Al Capone — go to 126
Albert Einstein — go to 158

99. You've trailed Nosmo King to Great Yarmouth, a fishing village on the east coast of England. But

though there's plenty of catch here, King isn't about to be hooked. There's no sign of him, so you have to give up and go to 54.

100. It's 1960 when you reach Washington, D.C., and talk to John F. Kennedy. Just four years ago he wrote *Profiles In Courage,* and he's now the President of the United States. Sadly, you know that in 1963 he will be assassinated on a visit to Dallas. Right now, though, he agrees to talk to you, and you find him a friendly and cheery man. You ask him about the thief you're after.

"You know," he tells you, "she did come by here. But the Secret Service men chased her away because she looked very suspicious. Sorry I can't be of more help."

Well, at least you know you're getting close. Time to head back to base (96) and try another of your leads.

101. Michaelangelo Buonarroti was known not only for his painting but also for his sculpture, his architecture, and even his poetry. You find him in Rome, at the Vatican, where he has recently finished his marble *Pieta*. He's taking a rest before he heads off to Florence, where he'll spend four years carving his statue of *David*. Later, he'll spend more years painting the roof of the Sistine Chapel.

He remembers seeing the thief you're hunting. "A red-haired man," he tells you. "He stopped by to admire my work. Then he had to leave. He said he had an appointment to meet a man called Cortes, and he didn't want to be late."

You thank him for his help and wish him luck with his new statue. Then you head back to base (69) to check out these leads.

102. George Stephenson is at the peak of his inventiveness in this year of 1825. In northern England, he's just finished building the first line on which steam locomotives will run. His new train, the *Locomotion*, can travel at speeds of up to fifteen miles per hour! In four years time, his most famous engine, the Rocket, will double that speed. Right now, though, he's feeling rather proud of himself and is quite happy to stop work to chat with you.

"Yes, I recall that brown-eyed man," he tells you. "He was annoyed at the noise my locomotive makes, and so he left. Said he was off to hear the most beautiful piece of music ever written, *Ode to Joy*. I told him that I'd borrowed five shillings from one of my neighbors, and that was what was owed to Joy. He didn't seem to think it was very funny."

Neither do you, but you smile and thank him. Then you head back to the Chronoskimmer (130) before he can crack any more bad jokes.

103. You've arrived in France, and the year is 1928. It's a time of peace and prosperity, with the damage of World War One now a part of the past. Life is getting better, and people are cheerier. No one can see that in eleven years, France will be crushed again by another German invasion.

Still, right now, everything is fine. The chronoskimmer's computer tells you that the villain you're after met with three people before traveling on. The crook might have gone to any of three destinations.

If you want to question:
Madame Curie — go to 38
Alphonse Mucha — go to 107
Maurice Ravel — go to 79

If you're ready to move to:
Italy in the year 1472 — go to 1
Holland in the year 1660 — go to 55
Holland in the year 1870 — go to 87

104. Alexander III is the pope in 1174, but he's by no means a peaceful man. Leading the armies of Italy, he will finally defeat Barbarossa in two years' time. Right now, though, Alexander is working on upcoming battles. He takes a few

moments to talk to you, and you ask him about the theft of the Leaning Tower of Pisa.

"Ah, a sad deed," he replies. "I did hear that the woman who stole the tower was going to hear a performance of *The Four Seasons*."

You head back to your Chronoskimmer (80) to check out this new information.

105. You're in London, England, in this war-torn year of 1066. Not only will William the Conqueror land in the south this year, but a Viking army will attack in the north. These are troubled times for the island of Britain, and if the crown jewels aren't recovered, times will get even worse.

The chronoskimmer's computer in your Chronoskimmer stops humming and beeps to let you know it's finished checking the energy patterns in the air. It has figured out that the theft was seen by three people and that the thief escaped in a time machine to one of three times and places. If you talk to the witnesses, they may help you figure out where the crook has gone.

If you want to talk to:
William the Conqueror — go to 11
Hereward the Wake — go to 48
Edward the Confessor — go to 97

If you're ready to move to:
America in the year 1799 — go to 161
Spain in the year 1501 — go to 137
America in the year 1900 — go to 57

106. You are now in America, and the year is 1875. The Civil War has been over for ten years, and some of the bitterness if finally dying out. To show that things are improving in the South, the very first Kentucky Derby horserace is held this year. Maybe the thief is here to try and fix the race!

Your chronoskimmer's computer beeps, telling you it's ready. The crook met three people here and then went on to one of three possible times and places.

If you want to meet:
Frederic Remington — go to 37
Sitting Bull — go to 4
Thomas Alva Edison — go to 82

If you're ready to travel to:
Italy in the year 1322 — go to 118
Italy in the year 1269 — go to 66
China in the year 1282 — go to 162

107. You find Alphonse Mucha hard at work in his Paris studio. Though he was born in Czechoslovakia,

he did all of his important work in France. Mucha is best known for his prints and posters of beautiful women with long, curling hair and flowers. He also helped create Art Nouveau ("New Art"). When Mucha stops painting to talk with you, you ask about the thief you're tracking.

"Yes, I saw the woman you seek," he tells you. "She wanted to work for me as a model. I told her that I have plenty of models. So she left, saying something about wanting to read a book about the life and death of Ivan the Terrible."

As he returns to his painting, you head back to base (103) to check out this clue.

108. You've trailed Scar Graynolt to a trailer park in the middle of nowhere. The trail's gone cold here, and there's nothing left for you to do but to go to 54.

109. Francisco Pizarro turns out to be a greedy and unpleasant man. He scowls at you, wanting to know why you're here. You can see how he will become one of the cruelest of all Spanish invaders of America and also how he could bring himself to destroy the Inca Empire in Peru. Fighting down your dislike of him, you ask about the criminal you're after.

"Yes, I saw him," Pizarro tells you. "A fool, if

ever I saw one. He told me he was going on from here to meet a French king. I don't know why he'd want to do that, and I don't much care."

You're glad to get away from him — and to return to base (61) to follow up this lead.

110. You've trailed Carmen Sandiego herself to the set of a Hollywood movie musical. But when you arrive, the place is crowded. There's no sign of Carmen. She's slipped past you again! Well, the only thing you can do now is to head to 54.

111. Baruch Spinoza was a famous and influential philosopher best known for his belief that God is part of everything that exists. Spinoza wrote many books and made a lot of enemies with his ideas. But he welcomes you politely to his home, and you ask him about the crook you're trailing.

"She did stop by to see me," he tells you. "But she seemed to be in a rush. When she left, she told me she had tickets for a performance of *Romeo And Juliet* and didn't want to be late for the start."

You thank him for his help and return to your Chronoskimmer (55) to check out your information.

112. You have arrived in America in 1927. This year *The Jazz Singer*, starring Al Jolson, will

become the first ever talking — and singing — movie. But you're not singing. There's no sign at all of the crook you're after, so you head to 17.

113. Joseph Turner is considered to be one of the greatest landscape painters of all time. He created more than twenty thousand paintings, most of which explore the use of light. As you arrive at his house, you see that the door is slightly open. Suspicious . . . When you look inside, you see that there's a man taking paintings from the studio.

One of Carmen's gang at work! Quietly, you slip in and tap the thief on the shoulder. He tries to pull a gun on you, but a quick karate chop disarms him and another lays him out cold on the floor.

Quickly, you search him, and you strike gold. In his pocket is a list of the names and addresses of all of Carmen's gang! The person who stole the crown jewels has to be on this list.

If you think the thief is:
Heidi Gosikh — go to 20
Pete Moss — go to 73
Sybil Servant — go to 129
Fast Eddie B — go to 165
Nosmo King — go to 3
Lady Agatha Wayland — go to 157
Carmen Sandiego — go to 141

114. You arrive at Peking, the newly created capital of China, where Kublai Khan has his palace. Kublai Khan is the grandson of Genghis Khan, and he's a very different kind of person from his grandfather. Quiet and thoughtful, Kublai Khan is one of the finest rulers China ever knew. He encouraged both art and science and worked to make the country into a great power. He allows you to speak with him, and you ask him about the crook you're chasing.

"He was here," the Khan tells you. "But I would not see him. He then left, and my guards tell me he mentioned that he was going off to see a scientist."

You thank the Khan politely and hurry back to your Chronoskimmer (162) to follow up on this clue.

115. Georg Frederic Handel was born in Germany, but he moved to England in 1712 and became vastly popular. You've trailed Sybil Servant to a performance of one of his newest pieces, the *Water Music*. It's being played on a boat that is tied to a dock. When you spot Sybil, you tap her on the shoulder.

"The game's up," you tell her. "Time to face the music."

"Stupid gumshoe!" she snarls, trying to make a run for it. You stick out a foot, and she trips, falling over the side of the boat and into the Thames River. You find a pole and use it to pull her out. "Face it, Sybil," you tell her. "You're all washed up."

You take her back with you to the present day to recover the stolen dodo. After you turn her over to the police, you call the Chief to let him know that you've solved another case.

"Excellent work," he tells you. "Why not head straight to the back of the book to see if you earned your promotion?"

116. This is England in the year 1595, and the country is doing very well. The defeat of the Spanish Armada in 1588 made other countries steer clear of trouble with England. Queen Elizabeth is nearing the end of her long and popular reign, and writers like Shakespeare and Edmund Spenser are creating classic works.

Your chronoskimmer's computer tells you it's finished checking the energy trails left by the crook. The thief spoke to three people and then moved on to one of three possible places and times.

If you want to meet:
William Shakespeare — go to 88
Sir Francis Drake — go to 132
Queen Elizabeth — go to 19

If you're ready to travel to:
Russia in the year 1892 — go to 31
America in the year 1927 — go to 112
England in the year 1601 — go to 156

117. You've arrived in Italy in the year 1675. The country is still split into many small states, each trying to outdo the others. There are lots of small wars causing much unhappiness. Some of the unhappiness is yours, because there's no sign of the crook you're after. Time to move on to 17.

118. You've arrived in Italy in the year 1322. The plague known as the Black Death will be starting soon, and it will kill almost a quarter of the people in Europe. It's not a good time to be here — and there's no sign of the villain you're after. You travel on to 17.

119. You have to take a short side trip to India to meet with Rudyard Kipling, who is still working there as a reporter. He's gathering a lot of material for his books, many of which will become very famous. As well as writing two *Jungle Books*, Kipling will also write *Kim* and many poems and short stories. As a reporter, though, he's used to looking and taking notes about all that happens. You ask him about the thief you're

trailing.

"She was here for a while," he tells you. "But she found it boring. Strange lady. She said she was off to hear a performance of the *Bolero*. Whatever that is."

You head back to base (127) to check out this clue.

120. Richard Wagner is considered to be one of the greatest opera composers ever to have lived in Germany. He wrote *The Flying Dutchman*, for example, but it is for *The Ring Cycle* that he is best known. *The Ring Cycle* is made up of four different operas that tell one complete story. A performance of the complete *Ring* lasts over thirteen hours! That's too much for you, but Wagner is happy with it. He agrees to meet you, as long as you ask him for his autograph. He's almost as vain as he is musical!

You ask him about the crook you're trailing.

"A lovely lady," he tells you. "She thinks my work is wonderful. And she's right, of course. I said that my music makes you feel like you are flying. She told me that where she's off to next she really will be able to fly."

You thank him for his help — and for his autograph — and rush back to base (43) before he wants you to sit through one of his operas!

71

121. You arrive at the court of Queen Isabella of Spain. She rules the country with her husband, Ferdinand, and the two of them are very good at it. They gave Columbus the money to go exploring, and he discovered America for them. She later led the fight to free Grenada from invaders. You ask Isabella about the crook you're after.

"I saw him," she tells you. "He told me that he admired strong women and that, after this, he was going to get the autograph of another famous woman. Then I caught him trying to steal some of my jewels. I sent my soldiers after him, but he managed to get away."

You thank her for her help and head back to base (61) to check out this clue.

122. You've trailed Sybil Servant to the growing town of Los Angeles. With the rise of Hollywood, this once-sleepy area is getting bigger every day. But for all of that, it's not big enough to hide Sybil — if she was here. There's no sign of her, so you head off to 54.

123. Mulay Ismael was the Sultan of Morocco at a time when the small country was not doing too well. He was a good ruler, though, and managed to strengthen the country for a short while. You arrive at his palace, and he agrees to see you. You

ask him about the thief you're after.

"She did stop by here," he agrees. "She didn't stay long, though. Said she had to meet a famous soldier."

You head back to your Chronoskimmer (18) to check out this clue.

124. You've tracked Carmen Sandiego to Las Vegas. As the gambling capital of the world, you know that there's plenty of money and crime in this city. It's just the place where you'd bet Carmen would be hiding. But that's one bet you'd lose, because there's no sign of her here. You have to pack up and head for 54 — now.

125. You've arrived in America in the year 1525. Giovanni de Verrazano is leading a French party into where modern New York City stands. These are the first Europeans to come this far. You could do with some of Verrazano's guidance, because there's no sign of the crook you're after. You have to go 17.

126. Chicago is in the grip of gang warfare, and Al Capone is struggling to take over the entire city. He's a tough character who likes to pretend he's just an average businessman. After he takes one look at you, he knows you're a detective. He

turns on the charm, pretending he's not a crook.

"So," he asks carefully, "what does the gumshoe want with me?"

"I'm looking for a thief," you tell him.

Capone laughs. "This town's full of them. Some in jail, some running the town. Take your pick."

"The one I'm after stole the Liberty Bell," you tell him.

"So?" he asks. "Am I supposed to cry? Or rat on a fellow . . . businessman? Maybe you'd better go, gumshoe, before my boys get itchy trigger fingers." He snaps his fingers, and two thugs walk into the office. You can take a hint. Watching the three crooks, you back out of the room and head for the Chronoskimmer (98). You should have figured Capone would never tell a detective about another crook. But there are still other leads to follow.

127. You're in England, and the year is 1885. Queen Victoria is ruling the country, and progress is booming. Not only are subway trains being built, but science is on the rise, and music and literature are all the rage.

The computer in your Chronoskimmer beeps to tell you it's ready with its results. The crook spoke to three people, and there are three possible places the thief might have gone.

If you want to interrogate:
Sir H. Rider Haggard — go to 50
Rudyard Kipling — go to 119
Sir Arthur Sullivan — go to 22

If you think the theif went to:
America in the year 1937 — go to 67
France in the year 1880 — go to 151
France in the year 1928 — go to 103

128. You've reached America, and the year is 1892. People are coming to America from all over the world, and most of them are passing through the new Ellis Island complex in New York Harbor. But the crook you're after isn't among them, and neither should you be. Time to go to 17.

129. You're on the track of Sybil Servant, deep in the area called The Potteries. Much of the beautiful porcelain tableware comes out of this part of the country. There's plenty of fine china here, but no sign at all of Sybil. Finally, you give up and head to 54.

130. This is England in the year 1825. Napoleon has been defeated and has died in exile. Peace has come again to Europe, and English power is riding

high. But there's an unpopular king on the throne, George IV, and he doesn't care how much the people dislike him.

Still, you're not here to meet the king. The chronoskimmer's computer in the Chronoskimmer beeps to finish its work. It tells you that the crook you're chasing met with three people. And there are three places and times the thief may have gone to from here.

If you want to speak to:

John Constable — go to 33

George Stephenson — go to 102

The Duke of Wellington — go to 166

If you're ready to move to:

France in the year 1880 — go to 58

France in the year 1860 — go to 138

America in the year 1776 — go to 21

131. This is England, and the year is 1650. It's a time of war and unhappiness. King Charles has been executed, and the government is run by Oliver Cromwell, who uses his soldiers to enforce unpopular laws — like the banning of Christmas celebrations. It's not a good time to visit, and the crook you're after isn't here. Better go on to 17.

132. You find Sir Francis Drake in the small port of Exmouth, where he's playing a game of

bowls before he sets off on what will be his last voyage. One of the most famous sailors in England, Drake has made a bold trip around the world and has helped to defeat the Spanish Armada. When he finishes his game, you ask him about the thief you're after.

"Yes, I saw her," he tells you. "A strange lady, I think. She did mention that from here she was going to see a performance of *The Nutcracker* — whatever that may be."

"It's a ballet," you tell him. "Written by a Russian."

"Odd," he laughs. "With all of their cold, you'd think it would be an icebreaker and not a nutcracker they'd want!"

As he starts another game, you leave and head back to base (116) to follow up on your lead.

133. You're in England, and the year is 1845. Queen Victoria is on the throne, and it's a time of progress. Science is helping to tame the world, and new inventions seem to be coming daily. It's a time of change and improvements for many.

The chronoskimmer's computer finishes scanning the energy levels and tells you that the crook you're looking for is still in this time and country. There are three people the villain met.

If you want to investigate:

Charles Darwin — go to 40
Queen Victoria — go to 153
Joseph Turner — go to 113

134. Philadelphia in the year of 1752 is a busy place. It's very much the unofficial capital of America, which is still a part of England at this time. But some are saying that America should be free of all ties to England, and there's a revolution not too far in the future. Right now, though, there's little to show of that.

The computer in your Chronoskimmer beeps and tells you that the thief met with three people here, and that he or she then escaped. It could be to one of three possibilities, but if you question the people the crook met, maybe you can narrow things down.

To talk to:

Benjamin Franklin — go to 86
Paul Revere — go to 41
John Hancock — go to 62

If you think the thief has fled to:
France in the year 1892 — go to 154
England in the year 1825 — go to 130
England in the year 1703 — go to 16

135. You arrive at the home of Jesse James, only to find he's a child of three! Looking at the

cute little fellow, it's hard to believe that one day he'll grow up to be one of the most feared bank and train robbers of all time. He's so quiet and good now. But can he help you? You ask him if he's seen any strangers here, and he points at you.

"Apart from me," you explain.

"Saw one lady," he tells you. "Sang a song to me." He starts to hum, and you recognize the tune — it's *The Blue Danube*. "Said she was gonna go dancing."

You thank him for his help and set off for your base (71) to check out this clue.

136. You find Neil Armstrong in the Air Force. He's flying planes, getting ready to make his future trip into space, during which he will become the first person to step on the moon. Right now, though, he's a cheery young man who waves at you at his plane takes off.

Well, this was a dead end. He's going to be gone for hours. Better use the time wisely and head back to the Chronoskimmer (96) to follow up on another lead.

137. You've reached Spain in the year 1501. It's too early for their best years — later on this century Cervantes will write *Don Quixote*, and El Greco will start a strong new line in art. After you

79

discover that the crook you want isn't here, you head to 17.

138. This is France, and the year is 1860. Louis Pasteur is working hard to try and cure diseases. But it'll be a while before his theories about tiny creatures called germs will be accepted. And it'll be a while before you realize that you're in the wrong place and that you should make your way to 17.

139. When you find Daniel Defoe, you learn that he is a retired merchant who is about to create the modern English novel. He's just finished work on *Robinson Crusoe* when you arrive at his house. It's a good thing you arrived when you did, for there's a crook in the house!

Thinking quickly, you pick up a vase and throw it at the gunman. It hits his arm, and he drops his gun. Quickly for a man of his age, Defoe jumps the crook and gives him a punch to the jaw. With crossed eyes, the robber collapses. He's out cold.

"Defoe beats the foe!" the old man laughs. "Thanks to your timely help." He shakes your hand. "This scoundrel was after my book, and it's due at the printer's today!"

Obviously, the villain was one of Carmen's gang.

You're certainly on the right track now. As Defoe hurries off to the printer's with his finished book, you hurry back to the Chronoskimmer (9) to follow another lead.

140. Alessandro Volta is in his laboratory when you arrive. He's working on improving what is known as the Voltaic Pile. It's the world's first electric battery, but doesn't look much like the ones you put into your tape player. Instead, it's a jar with two large rods in it and with wires running out of it. Volta greets you as you arrive, and you ask him about the crook you're trailing.

"She was here a short while ago," he tells you. "She said she needed batteries for her flashlight — whatever that may be."

"Any idea where she might have gone?" you ask.

"She did say she wanted to read Utopia ," he replies.

Thanking him, you head back to the Chronoskimmer (14) to check out this lead.

141. You've tracked Carmen Sandiego to a large building in London — which turns out to be the infamous Newgate Prison! You don't expect to find her here, and the warden agrees that she's not one of the prisoners. Sighing, you head off to 54.

142. Phags-Pa turns out to be a Tibetan monk. Kublai Khan has given him the task of making up a Mongolian alphabet so that he can write books in his own language. Though the alphabet won't ever catch on, it does help inspire the writing of many books. You ask the monk about the crook you're trying to catch.

"Ah, he was here," Phags-Pa replies. "But he didn't stay long. He said it was too quiet here and that he was going off to hear a performance of the Bolero."

You thank him for his help and leave him working on his alphabet. Time to head back to base (162) and check out this new lead.

143. You're in France in the year 1422. There's an English invasion going on, and the country is torn by war. You're not too happy about that — or about the fact that there's no sign of your robber. Time to get to 17.

144. Anton Chekhov turns out to be a writer of short stories, and his real fame as a writer of plays is just a few years in the future. Although he'll have a big influence on twentieth-century writers, at the moment Chekhov isn't too well known. He stops his work to welcome you, and you ask about

the thief you're tracking.

"Ah, that brown-eyed lady," he smiles. "A strange person. She wanted my autograph, and when I asked if she collected them, and she said that she did. Told me she was going to get Wagner's next."

You wish him well with his writing and head back to base (31) to check out his information.

145. You arrive in Domremy, France, where Joan of Arc is feeding pigs on a farm. In two years, however, she will be leading a French army into battle against English invaders. You go up to her and ask about the villain you're tracking.

"I saw him," she tells you. "He was trying to steal some food from the kitchen. I boxed his ears and sent him running!"

"Do you have any idea where he might have gone?" you ask her.

"Well, he did say something about wanting to see an English queen," she tells you. "What a scoundrel — who could like the English when they invade our land like this?" She thinks for a moment. "Oh, yes — he was wearing a large ring on his little finger."

Thanking her for her help, you head back to your Chronoskimmer (32) to check out this new information.

146. You've trailed Lady Agatha Wayland to a party at the home of John Rockefeller in New York City. But when you arrive, the butler tells you she isn't here. He coldly suggests that you take a trip to 54.

147. You arrive at the studio of Rembrandt van Rijn in Amsterdam. He's hard at work on one of his large, richly colored paintings, but he's glad to take a short break to talk with you. After admiring the beauty of his work, you ask about the thief you're after.

"She was here," he tells you. "She wanted me to paint her picture. She had nice gray eyes, but I told her I was all booked up for the next few years. As she left, she mentioned that she was going to be seeing a pirate soon."

You head back to base (55) to check out this new information.

148. Bonanno Pisano is the man who designed the Leaning Tower of Pisa. He didn't do his homework because its foundation wasn't very secure! To this day, the tower does not standing straight. When you arrive, Bonanno is in a nervous mood.

"It's not my fault," he starts to say. "It's that silly building firm we hired."

"Relax," you tell him. "I'm not here about the

plans for the tower. I'm trailing the thief that stole it."

"I saw her as she was leaving," he tells you. "She has black hair, and I heard her say something about getting Dumas' autograph. Do you think you can get my tower back?"

"I think so," you tell him.

"Maybe you could bring it back straightened up?" he asks. "The council of Pisa isn't too happy with it as it is."

"Don't worry," you tell him. "It's going to be the most famous building in the city one day. Trust me." You head back to your Chronoskimmer (80).

149. You're in America in the year 1875. The railroad has now joined east and west, and the Civil War is ten years past. The United States is becoming a single country in more and more ways. But that's not much help to you, because there's no sign of the crook you're after. You'd better go to 17.

150. Claude Monet is in his house outside of Paris, where he's studying the flowers. His painting *Impression: Sunrise* was the first in a style of painting called Impressionism. In this style, the artist is more interested in capturing the mood and feel of a subject rather than in painting it

true to life. As you arrive, Monet looks up from his water lilies, and you ask about the thief you're after.

"He was here earlier today," Monet replies. "Said he was interested in painting, but when I showed him my works, he said he didn't care for them. He mentioned liking the paintings of Remington and then said that he was going to see him at work."

You head back to base (58) to check out this information.

151. You're in France, and the year is 1880. It's a good time for art, and painters like Cezanne and Gaughin are very popular. But not with you — because there's no sign of the crook you're looking for. You head to 17.

152. You've trailed Fast Eddie B to Alaska, which was made the forty-ninth state only last year. But there's no sign of him here. The trail is definitely cold! You head off to 54 as fast as you can!

153. You arrive at Buckingham Palace, the home of Queen Victoria. She became queen at the age of seventeen and would rule for sixty-four years. She was a popular queen, but very stub-

born with her own ideas of what to do. She allows you in to see her, and you ask her about the thief you're hunting.

"Yes, that scoundrel was here," she tells you. "He was trying to trick me out of some of my jewels. When I threatened to throw him in the Tower of London, he said that he was only joking. I told him that I was not amused, and he left in a hurry."

You thank her for her help and head back to your Chronoskimmer (133) to take up another of your leads.

154. You've arrived in France in the year 1892. There's a big move on to take large parts of West Africa, and everyone seems to be heading out to explore or work there. But there's no sign of the crook you're trailing, and you head to 17.

155. Maurice of Nassau is the Dutch landowner for whom the island of Mauritius was named. This seems a little odd, since he never actually visited the place! You find Maurice at his home in Holland, where you ask him about the thief you're after.

"She did stop by here," he tells you. "Said something about being on her way to see a president, and then she left."

You thank him for his help and head back to

your Chronoskimmer (18) to check out this lead.

156. This in England, and the year is 1601. The long reign of Queen Elizabeth will soon come to an end — but your hunt won't. There's no sign of the villain you're chasing, so you have to move on to 17.

157. You've trailed Lady Agatha Wayland to the country estate of some lord or other. But when you arrive, the gatesmen tell you she isn't here. They threaten to set the dogs on you if you hang around. You can take a hint and head straight to 54.

158. You arrive at the home of the famous scientist Albert Einstein. He's scribbling away at some calculations in his book when you arrive. You ask him about the crook you're after, but he doesn't remember seeing him.

"I get so caught up in my work," he explains. "I'm sorry I can't help."

A dead end here. But you head back to the Chronoskimmer (98) to check out another of your leads.

159. You've reached England, and the year is 1547. The king is Henry VIII, who is famous for

having six wives and for splitting the church in England from the Pope in Rome. It's time for you to split, too, because the crook you're trailing isn't here. Head straight to 17.

160. You're in France, and the year is 1921. World War One is over, and the country is struggling back to its feet. You're struggling, too, because there's no sign of the thief you're after. You give up and go to 17.

161. You've arrived in America, and the year is 1799. There's trouble with France. French ships are raiding American ships at sea, and America has retaliated by allowing privateers, or legal pirates, to raid French shipping. Before it comes to all-out war, though, Napoleon comes to power in France and orders the raiding stopped.

Your chronoskimmer's computer comes up with the information you need. The crook met three people and then left this time and country. There are three possible places the thief might have gone, so you'd better start digging up clues!

If you want to talk to:

Benedict Arnold — go to 44
George Washington — go to 93
Washington Irving — go to 15

If you think the crook went to:
Italy in the year 1675 — go to 117
American in the year 1875 — go to 149
Italy in the year 1514 — go to 69

162. You've reached China in the year 1282. The Mongol hordes have taken over the whole country, and Kublai Khan is in charge. He's a clever ruler, who has welcomed the Italian traveler Marco Polo to help him out. Your chronoskimmer's computer beeps to let you know it's finished checking the energy patterns. The crook you want met three people, and there are three places he or she could have gone.

If you want to question:
Marco Polo — go to 78
Kublai Khan — go to 114
Phags-Pa — go to 142

If you're ready to move to:
America in the year 1910 — go to 53
America in the year 1930 — go to 98
France in the year 1920 — go to 25

163. You've trailed Pete Moss to a country garden. But when you get there, the trail is cold. There's no sign of him, so you have to give up and go to 54.

164. Count Leo Tolstoy owns a big estate just outside of Moscow, where he works away at his stories. One of the great Russian writers, Tolstoy is best known for the books *War And Peace* and *Anna Karenina*. He stops his work to chat with you, though, and you ask him about the crook you're trailing.

"She was here," he tells you. "She had big, brown eyes, and asked for my autograph. She said she collects them and aimed to get her copy of *Rip Van Winkle* signed next."

You thank him for his help and then head back to base (31) to check out this lead.

165. You've trailed Fast Eddie B to the workshops of Isambard Kingdom Brunel, the famous engineer. Brunel built steel bridges, laid railroads, and made huge steamships, like the *Great Eastern*. As you arrive, you spot Eddie making his way through the factory areas toward the big, steel safe in the office. You realize he's trying to steal the payroll!

He's working on getting the safe open when you creep up behind him and tap him on the shoulder. He jumps up, and you quickly snap a pair of handcuffs onto his wrists.

"If you like steel, Eddie," you tell him, "try these on for size!"

He sighs and looks down at the floor. "It's a fair cop," he agrees.

You take him with you back to the present day and see him off to jail. The police find the crown jewels and return them to their right place and time. With the case all wrapped up, you give the Chief a call and tell him the good news.

"Great work," he exclaims. "I just knew you'd be the person to crack this one. Well, head for the back of the book and see if you've earned yourself a promotion!"

166. The Duke of Wellington is the soldier who finally managed to defeat Napoleon. Known by his men as "the Iron Duke," he's now a member of the government. In a few years, he'll become Prime Minister of England. You ask him about the crook you're hunting.

"I saw the villain," he tells you. "He mentioned that he wanted to meet Offenbach, a French composer. After telling him he should stick to British composers instead, I threw the scoundrel out."

You decide to retreat before he throws you out, too. You head back to base (130) to follow up on this clue.

167. You've trailed Carmen Sandiego herself

to a small country house just outside of London. But here the trail ends, and you're left without a clue. Eventually, you give up and head to 54.

168. You arrive at the home of Beethoven and welcomed in. To your surprise, you discover that the composer is totally deaf! In fact, when his most famous work, *Ode To Joy*, was first performed, he couldn't hear any of the applause for his genius. He didn't even know that the audience was applauding at all until one of the musicians turned him around on the stage to show him.

Beethoven is good at reading lips, though, and he understands you when you ask about the crook you're tracking.

"She came past here," he tells you. "Mentioned that she was going to pick up a copy of *Huckleberry Finn* to read."

You thank him for his help and leave him to continue his work. Time to head back to the Chronoskimmer (43) and follow up on this clue.

169. This is England in the year 1875. It's the age of transport, with steamships crossing the Atlantic Ocean to America and trains traveling all over the place. But you've traveled to the wrong place, and there's no sign here of the thief you want. You'd better move on to 17.

170. You're in the Antarctic, where Admiral Byrd is exploring and has already made a famous flight over the South Pole. As you arrive in the freezing cold, you spot someone going through the admiral's things.

One of Carmen's gang! Quickly, you run over. The robber hears you coming and tries to run away. But it's very slippery and he falls down, knocking himself out cold.

"One crook on ice," you laugh. As you start to go through his pockets, you find a piece of paper. You look it over and realize that you're hot on the trail! It's a list of the hideouts used by the members of Carmen's gang.

If you think that the thief you're after is:

Nosmo King — go to 45
Pete Moss — go to 8
Carmen Sandiego — go to 110
Scar Greynolt — go to 94
Sybil Servant — go to 122
Heidi Gosikh — go to 70
Lady Agatha Wayland — go to 146
Fast Eddie B — go to 29

SCORING CHART

Add up all of your travel points. (You did remember to mark one point for each time you moved to a new number, didn't you?) If you have penalty points for trying to arrest the wrong person, add those in, too. Then check your score against the chart below to see how you did.

0 – 17: You couldn't really have solved these cases in these few steps. Either you're boasting about your abilities or you're actually working with Carmen's gang. Be honest and try again —if you dare!

18 – 40: Super sleuth! You work very well and don't waste time. Well done — you deserve the new rank and the nice big bonus you'll get next payday!

41 – 60: Private eye material! You're a good, steady worker, and you get your man (or woman). Still, there's room for improvement, and you can always try again to get another promotion.

61 – 80: Detective first class. You're not a world-famous private eye yet, but you're getting there. Try again and see if you can move up a grade or two!

81 – 100: Rookie material. You're taking too long to track down the crooks. Next time they're going to get away from you. Try a little harder and see if you're really better than this.

Over 100: Are you sure you're really cut out to be a detective? Maybe you'd be better off looking for an easier job — a janitor for Acme, maybe? Still, if you're determined to be a detective, why not try again and see if this was just an off day. Better luck next time!